PUG MEETS PIG

For Terry, Katherine, Matt, Becca, and Jackson,
and all of my book-loving family—S. L. G.

For Teresa, who always helps me out
whenever I'm stuck—J. W.

ISBN 978-1-338-22205-0

12 11 10 9 8 7 6 5 4 3 2 1   17 18 19 20 21 22

Printed in the U.S.A.   40

First Scholastic printing, September 2017

Book design by Lauren Rille
The text for this book is set in Baker Street.
The illustrations for this book are rendered in pencil and then colored digitally.

written by
Sue Lowell Gallion

PUG
MEETS
PIG

PUG

illustrated by
Joyce Wan

SCHOLASTIC INC.

This is Pug's home.
This is where Pug lives.

This is Pug's bowl.
This is where Pug eats.

This is Pug's yard.
This is where Pug works.

And this is Pug's bed.
This is where Pug sleeps.

Pug is happy here at home,
with his bowl, his yard, and his bed.

But one day when the door opens . . .

out trots someone new.

Pig meets Pug.

Pug meets Pig.

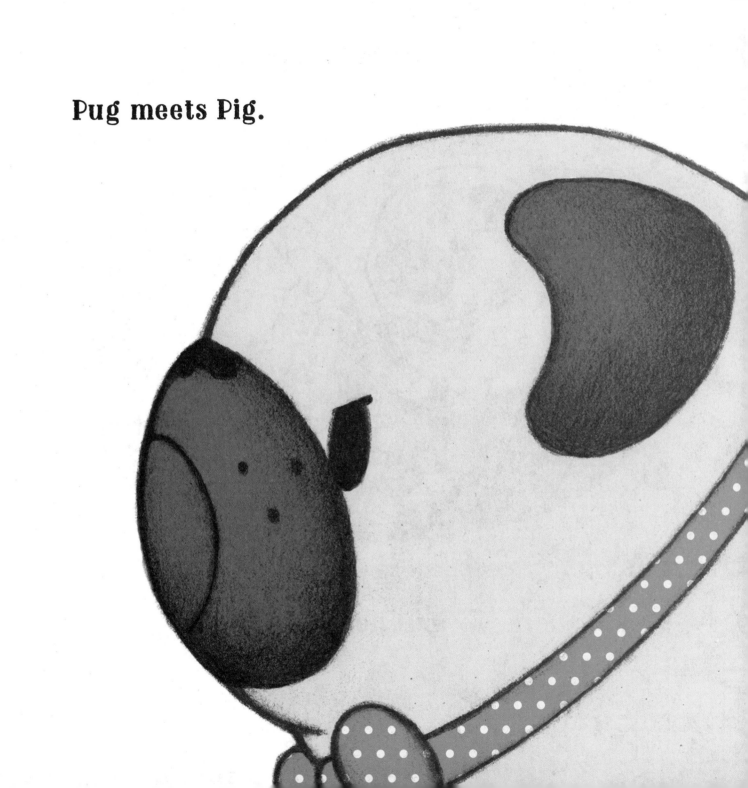

Pug is hungry.

But here is Pig.

arf! arf!
arf!

Pug has work to do.

But here is Pig.

Pug needs some sleep.

But here is Pig!

Pug is not happy.

He is not happy here at home anymore.

Pug cannot stay here.

He packs his things.

But wait!
What's this?

Now Pug can come and go without Pig!

Once again,
Pug is happy here at home.

But someone else is not . . .

Pig's head can fit
through the doggy door.

Pig's tail can fit
through the doggy door.

But Pig's round middle cannot fit.

What a sad Pig!

Perhaps Pug could help.

Perhaps Pug should help.

Perhaps Pug *will* help.

Pug scratches and gnaws.
He chews and claws.
And then the doggy
door for Pug . . .

is also a piggy door for Pig!

Now this is where Pug and Pig eat.

This is where Pug and Pig work.

This is where Pug and Pig sleep.

Pug is happy here at home . . .

and so is Pig.

SUE LOWELL GALLION has always loved dogs. When she was little, her family's dogs were dachshunds named Mitzi and Molly. Now a black lab mix named Tucker shares *his* Kansas City home with Sue and her family. Sue likes meeting new people and Tucker *usually* likes meeting new dogs. But he's never met a pig. Yet.

JOYCE WAN loves drawing animals—especially cute, round, and chubby ones—even though she's never been lucky enough to have a pet dog or pig of her own. She lives in Ridgewood, New Jersey, where she happily shares everything with her husband—except french fries.